For Ben,
friend and collaborator.
Thanks for bringing my
sketchy ideas to life.
—K.B.

For Kevin.
May my sketches always
live up to your ideas!
Thanks for everything, amigo.
—B.H.

One of the first and most important steps to becoming a reader is mastering basic sight words. These "sight words" are the most frequently used words in the language, the basic building blocks and connectors in every text children will encounter. So fluent readers need to recognize and read them automatically "on sight."

This book is designed to teach 53 of the very first of those sight words.

Kevin Bolger
Reading Specialist

Fun with Ed and Fred Copyright © 2016 by Kevin Bolger and Ben Hodson. All rights reserved. Manufactured in China. No part of this book may be used or reproduced in any manner whatsoever without written permission except in the case of brief quotations embodied in critical articles and reviews. For information address HarperCollins Children's Books, a division of HarperCollins Publishers, 195 Broadway, New York, NY 10007. www.harpercollinschildrens.com

Library of Congress Control Number: 2014958850
ISBN 978-0-06-228600-0

Book design by Victor Joseph Ochoa
15 16 17 18 19 SCP 10 9 8 7 6 5 4 3 2 1 ❖ First Edition

FUN with ED and FRED

by Kevin Bolger   illustrated by Ben Hodson

HARPER
An Imprint of HarperCollinsPublishers

This is Ed.

That is Fred.

Ed is at the beach.

Fred is not at the beach.

Ed plays on the beach.

Fred is not at the beach.

Ed runs.

Ed jumps.

Ed swims.

Fred is still not at the beach.

But
I can run.
I can jump.
I can swim.

Ed is on a horse.

Okay, Fred is on the horse.

The horse is on Fred.

Ed is in a red car.

Fred is yellow in a car.

Then Fred is blue.

Fred goes up.

Now this is more like it.

POP

Fred comes down.

Ed is over the water.

Fred is under the water.

Ed has a little dog.

A big dog has Fred.

Ed's dog is nice.

Fred's dog is not.

Ed is out of the tornado.

Fred is in the tornado.

Ed was there.

Fred was here.

Ed—

If you say so.

Fred sees a giant monster.

GRRAAAAWR...

The giant monster sees Fred.

Yikes! Hide me!

Look out, Fred!

Look out for that giant monster!

No, Fred. Not in there.

But . . .

Okay, have it your way.